Olaf Gives Thanks

Written by **Colin Hosten** • Illustrated by **Olga T. Mosqueda**

DISNEP PRESS

Los Angeles • New York

Olaf
is thankful
for all
of his
friends.

He **loves** spending time with them—

beginning to **end.**

Olaf is thankful
for his fun
carrot nose.
He **loves** it more
than anyone **knows!**

Olaf is thankful
for **trees**
and for **flowers.**

He stops to **sniff** them for **hours** and **hours**.

Olaf
is thankful
for **ice**
and for
SNOW.

They're the **reason**
his family
is able to
grow.

Olaf is thankful
for getting **warm hugs**.
From new friends and old,
they make him feel **loved**!

Olaf is thankful
for **music** so **sweet.**

He **sings** and he **dances**
on two **snowball** feet.

Olaf
is thankful
for **magic** and
laughter.

His **grand tales**
and stories
bring **smiles**
for hours after.

Olaf
is thankful
for the **cool**
summer
breeze.

It helps him
keep **cool**
under the
palm trees.

Olaf is thankful
for the
Northern Lights.

They're **pretty** to look at on **wintry** nights.

Olaf
is thankful
for **BIG** royal
feasts.

They bring
people together,
from the **west**
to the **east**.

Olaf gives thanks
for a great **many** things,

Especially the **wonders** that **each day** brings.

Dedicated to everyone who helps make the **magic** happen every day, and for whom I am deeply grateful. —C.H.

Dedicated to my sweet boy **Jeremy**. I give thanks for you. —O.T.M.

Printed in the United States of America

First Hardcover Edition, October 2018

Library of Congress Control Number: 2017963709

1 3 5 7 9 10 8 6 4 2

ISBN 978-1-368-02320-7

FAC-038091-18229

For more Disney Press fun, visit www.disneybooks.com

SUSTAINABLE FORESTRY INITIATIVE · Certified Sourcing · www.sfiprogram.org · SFI-00993 · **Logo Applies to Text Stock Only**